Primary
D
c.1

Dumas, Philippe
The story of Edward
X54376

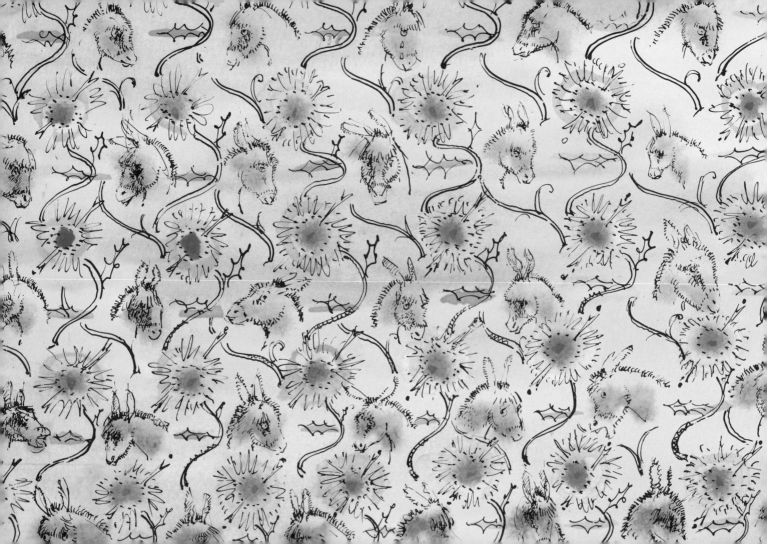

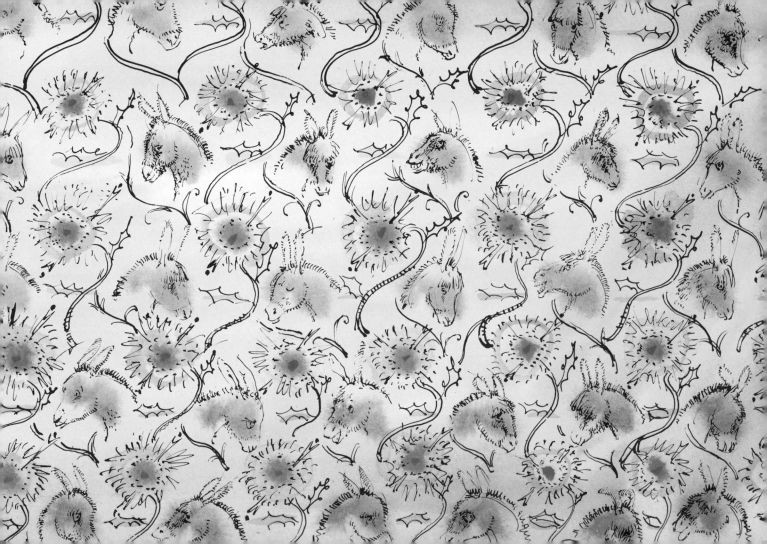

THE STORY OF EDWARD

Philippe Dumas

Parents' Magazine Press · New York

For Elsie and David C. Fender

Translated from *Histoire d'Edouard*
copyright © Flammarion, 1976
English translation copyright © J. M. Dent & Sons Limited and Parents' Magazine Press, 1977
All rights reserved. Printed in Great Britain.

Library of Congress Cataloging in Publication Data

Dumas, Philippe.
   The story of Edward.
   Translation of Histoire d'Edouard.
   SUMMARY: The adventures of a clever donkey with a talent for waltzing.
   [1. Donkeys—Fiction] I. Title.
PZ7.D8935St [E] 76-28720
ISBN 0–8193–0868–4 ISBN 0–8193–0869–2 lib. bdg.

This is a story with a happy ending about a donkey called Edward.

Here is Edward dancing a waltz. He has a wonderful talent for waltzing.

And here is Edward's old master, Angelo Dupas,
a musician of remarkable skill.

It was Angelo Dupas who taught Edward to waltz.

Together they put on a spectacular show.

They performed in village squares to enthusiastic crowds
who generously tossed coins into Angelo's hat.

At night they went to bed early, the better to enjoy their well-earned rest.

Each morning they would set off for another village.
Because he was so good-natured, Edward never minded playing
the donkey, though this role had little to do with dancing.

But one day the old musician felt too tired to go on.

"Edward," said Angelo, "you are quite able to manage on your own by now.
Take my money and all my belongings. You have been a good donkey and I wish you luc[k].
Just remember one thing: never let anybody see your long ears."

After doing what had to be done, Edward set off to seek his fortune.

But he was careful to keep his ears well hidden under his hat.

On he went, following his nose.

When he reached the next town he read the job advertisements in the local paper.

In time, he found work as a waiter at the Café Moderne.

It was a tiring job, but it paid well as long as you were quick
and did it with style—and remembered not to bray.

Unfortunately, the beautiful cashier—Mademoiselle Olive—was one of those creatures with whom everyone falls in love.

And so, one Saturday night, poor Edward threw all caution to the winds.
Rushing to open the door for her, he took off his hat, and bowed.

His secret had been discovered.

At dawn next day, two policemen came to take Edward away
and put him to work as a donkey.

Edward asked permission to put on his trousers.

Every exit was blocked by men in uniform.

In the street below, Edward could see the beautiful Mademoiselle Olive's carriage waiting for him to be harnessed between the shafts.

Edward escaped through a back window.

He raced towards the open countryside as fast as he could go.

For three whole days he continued his wanderings, thinking
gloomy thoughts under his hat.

On the morning of the fourth day he reached a small village.

What luck! He was offered a job.

Edward was very good at his new job . . .

. . . secretly using his hoofs to knock in the cobbles

. . . or trimming the roadside in his own special way.

But after his recent troubles, Edward was always on his guard.

Every day, however, an enchanting little white donkey passed
Edward on the road.

Edward saved up money out of his pay to buy her from her rough master.

The little white donkey wondered where her new master was taking her.

Soon Edward ordered her to stop. Climbing down from the wagon, he held her spellbound with these amazing words:

"Mademoiselle, for forty-two days I have been watching you go by.
My poor heart beats only for you.
You are the mistress of my fate and the object of my dreams."

"If only you will say yes, I would like to be your husband—
a suitable match because, as you see, I am a donkey, too."

40

They were married at once.

Edward and his charming bride disappeared
into the depths of the forest looking for a place to live.

They came upon an old deserted house and in no time turned it
into a model of comfort.

They are living there still, very happy, devoting themselves to the arts.

Of course, there are children, too . . .

. . . several little donkeys, each one more gifted and lively than the last.

In memory of his old master—Angelo Dupas, the musician—
and the good times they had, Edward gives everyone waltzing
lessons four times a week. There is nothing like dancing to create
family spirit—a fact worth noting before closing this book.

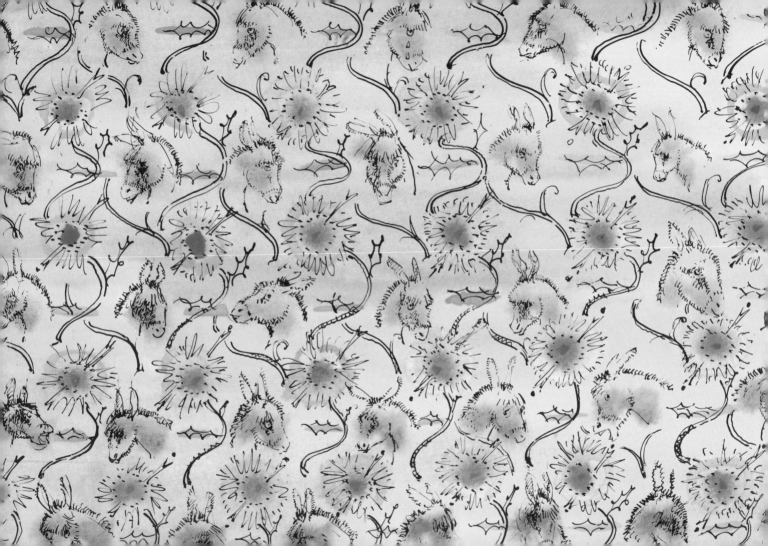

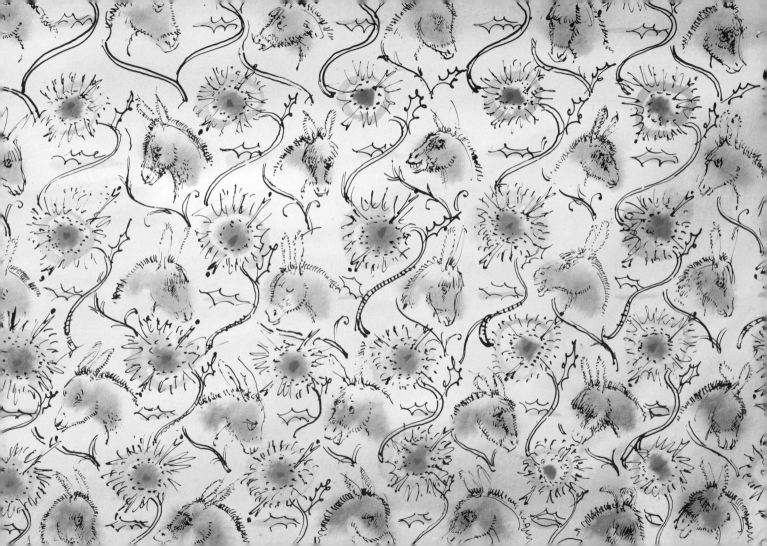